AF278355

Ohio State Murders

by Adrienne Kennedy

No one shall make any changes in this title(s) for the purpose of production. No part of this book may be reproduced, stored in a retrieval system, scanned, uploaded, or transmitted in any form, by any means, now known or yet to be invented, including mechanical, electronic, digital, photocopying, recording, videotaping, or otherwise, without the prior written permission of the publisher. No one shall share this title(s), or any part of this title(s), through any social media or file hosting websites.

For all inquiries regarding motion picture, television, online/digital and other media rights, please contact Concord Theatricals Corp.

MUSIC AND THIRD-PARTY MATERIALS USE NOTE

Licensees are solely responsible for obtaining formal written permission from copyright owners to use copyrighted music and/or other copyrighted third-party materials (e.g. artworks, logos) in the performance of this play and are strongly cautioned to do so. If no such permission is obtained by the licensee, then the licensee must use only original music and materials that the licensee owns and controls. Licensees are solely responsible and liable for clearances of all third-party copyrighted materials, including without limitation music, and shall indemnify the copyright owners of the play(s) and their licensing agent, Concord Theatricals Corp., against any costs, expenses, losses and liabilities arising from the use of such copyrighted third-party materials by licensees. For music, please contact the appropriate music licensing authority in your territory for the rights to any incidental music.

IMPORTANT BILLING AND CREDIT REQUIREMENTS

If you have obtained performance rights to this title, please refer to your licensing agreement for important billing and credit requirements.

OHIO STATE MURDERS was commissioned by the Great Lakes Theater Festival (Gerald Freedman, artistic director; Mary Bill, managing director) through a grant from the New Works Program of the Ohio Arts Council. The play received its world premiere at the Great Lakes Theater Festival on March 7, 1992. The production was directed by Gerald Freedman; set design conceived by Gerald Freedman and executed by John Ezell; projections by Kurt Sharp and Jesse Epstein; costumes coordinated by Al Kohout; lighting designed by Cynthia Stillings; sound design by Stanley M. Kozak with the following cast:

SUZANNE ALEXANDER . . . . .Ruby Dee

SUZANNE . . . . Bellary Darden

DAVID ALEXANDER . . . . Michael Early

ROBERT HAMPSHIRE . . . . .Allan Byrne

AUNT LOUISE . . . . .Irma Hall

VAL . . . . Rick Williams

IRIS ANN. . . . . Leslie Holland

SUZANNE'S FATHER . . . . Michael Early

The New York premiere of *OHIO STATE MURDERS* was produced by Theatre for a New Audience, Jeffrey Horowitz, Artistic Director; Theodore C. Rogers, Chairman; Dorothy Ryan, Managing Director, on October 27, 2007 at The Duke on 42nd StreetSM, a New 42nd Street® project. The production was directed by Evan Yionoulis, scenic design by Neil Patel, costume design by Emilio Sosa, lighting design by Christopher Akerlind, original music & sound design by Mike Yionoulis/Sarah Pickett, projection design by Leah Gelpe. The production stage manager was Linda Marvel, with assistant stage manager, Melissa M. Spengler. The cast was as follows:

SUZANNE ALEXANDER . . . . Lisagay Hamilton

SUZANNE . . . . .Cherise Boothe

ROBERT HAMPSHIRE . . . . Saxon Palmer

AUNT LOUISE . . . . .Aleta Mitchell

IRIS ANN. . . . . .Julia Pace Mitchell

DAVID ALEXANDER / VAL . . . . Kobi Libii

OHIO STATE MURDERS was part of the Signature Theatre Company's 1995-96 season devoted to Adrienne Kennedy.

CHARACTERS

SUZANNE ALEXANDER (1949-1952) – The young writer as a student attending Ohio State from 1949 to 1950

SUZANNE ALEXANDER (Present) – A well-known black writer visiting Ohio State to give a talk on the imagery in her work

DAVID ALEXANDER – A law student she will marry

ROBERT HAMPSHIRE – An English professor at Ohio State

MRS. TYLER – Suzanne's landlady

VAL – A friend

IRIS ANN – Suzanne's roommate

MISS DAWSON – Head of the dorm

TIME

Present.

SETTING

Night.

(Stacks: hundreds of books on "O" level beneath the library at Ohio State.

A window high in the distance from which can be seen University Hall, a vast dark structure and falling snow. The snow falls throughout the play.

Sections of the stacks become places on campus during the play.

SUZANNE *enters the stacks, wanders, gazes at the distant window and snow. She takes out a paper, studies it, gazes about her, reads from paper rehearsing a talk.)*

SUZANNE. *(Present)* I was asked to talk about the violent imagery in my work; bloodied heads, severed limbs, dead father, dead Nazis, dying Jesus. The chairman said, we do want to hear about your brief years here at Ohio State but we also want you to talk about violent imagery in your stories and plays. When I visited Ohio State last year it struck me as a series of disparate dark landscapes just as it had in 1949, the autumn of my freshman year.

I used to write down locations in order to learn the campus: the oval, behind the green, the golf hut, behind Zoology, the tennis courts beyond the golf hut, the Olitangy River, the stadium off to the right, the main library at the head of the Oval, the old union across from the dorm, High Street at the end of the path, downtown Columbus, the Deschler Wallach, Lazarus, the train station. The geography made me anxious.

The zigzagged streets beyond the Oval were regions of Law, Medicine, Mirror Lake, the Greek theater, the lawn behind the dorm where the white girls sunned.

The ravine that would be the scene of the murder and Mrs. Tyler's boarding house in the Negro district.

The music I remembered most was a song called "Don't Go Away Mad," and the music from *A Place in the Sun*, that movie with Elizabeth Taylor and Montgomery Clift based on Theodore Dreiser's *American Tragedy*.

(**SUZANNE** *takes out a picture of* **DAVID** *running the 100-yard dash at Ohio State.*

DAVID *is an extraordinarily handsome young black man. He looks like Frantz Fanon, whose biography he will one day write.*)

SUZANNE. *(Present)* This is a picture of my husband, David, who, as you know, is a writer, political activist, and biographer of Frantz Fanon. Most people don't know David started out as a lawyer.

Although we were both at Ohio State in the winter of 1950 I had not met David. But I had seen this photograph of him running the 100-yard dash at Ohio State's spring track meet.

I knew he was a state champion and now he was in law school. David had lived in the boarding house that was to become my home. Mrs. Tyler hung this picture in her hallway. She loved David Alexander. That was later.

But first I started my freshman year in the fall of '49.

I took a required English survey course although I was not an English major. I had declared no major course of study. We read Thomas Hardy.

(*SCENE:* Quonset hut. **HAMPSHIRE** *enters.* **SUZANNE** *[1949] watches him. As a student she wears pale skirt, sweater [powder blue], saddle shoes, and socks.*)

SUZANNE. *(Present)* The professor was a young man. His name was Hampshire. He was small and dressed rather formally in a tweed suit with a vest. He always walked straight to the lectern and without any introduction started his lectures.

(**HAMPSHIRE** *looks at his notes.* **SUZANNE** *[1949] watches him intently. She is fragile, pale.*)

The class was held in a quonset hut, a temporary barrack-like structure that had room for fifty to sixty students. These huts were built to house the overflow of students after the war. Professor Hampshire read from *Tess of the D'Urbervilles.*

HAMPSHIRE. "In spite of the unpleasant initiation of the day before, Tess inclined to the freedom and novelty of her new position in the morning when the sun shone, now that she was once installed there; and she was curious to test her powers in the unexpected direction asked of her, so as to ascertain her chance of retaining her post. As soon as she was alone within the walled garden she sat herself down on a coop, and seriously screwed up her mouth for the long-neglected practice. She found her former ability to have degenerated to the production of a hollow rush of wind through the lips and no clear note at all."

(**HAMPSHIRE** *draws a map.*)

SUZANNE. On a makeshift blackboard he drew a map of Wessex.

HAMPSHIRE. Blackmore Vale, Marlott, Edgdon Heath, New Forest, Chalk Newton, Casterbridge.

(**SUZANNE** *continues to watch him intently.*)

(*SCENE ENDS.*)

SUZANNE. *(Present) (Stands in stacks.)* These places in Wessex, Marlott, New Forest, Chalk Newton intrigued me as did *Tess of the D'Urbervilles.*

One afternoon late, almost early evening, I walked over behind the Oval to the English Department and inquired about the catalog for English majors. A secretary said, "Come back any morning around ten. A Miss Smith will give you the information about becoming an English major. What is your major now?" she asked.

I told her I was undeclared.

I didn't know there were no "Negro" students in the

English Department. It was thought that we were not able to master the program. They would allow you to take no more than two required freshman courses. After that you had to apply to the English Department to take courses that were all said to be for majors.

In my dorm across from the Old Union there were six hundred girls. Twelve of us were blacks. We occupied six places, rooming together two in a room.

The other dorms, Canfield and Neil, each also housed a few black girls.

The schools I had attended in Cleveland were an even mixture of immigrant and black. You were judged on grades. But here race was foremost.

Very few Negroes walked on High Street above the university. It wasn't that you were not allowed but you were discouraged from doing so. Above the university was a residential district encompassed by a steep ravine. I never saw this ravine until the two days I visited Bobby at his house (the ravine was where the faculty lived).

A year and a half later one of my baby twin daughters would be found dead there. That was later.

But in my freshman year the continuing happiness was Professor Hampshire's discussion of the Victorian novel.

When he lectured, his small pale face was expressionless. Only his blue eyes conveyed anger, joy, vitality.

(SCENE: Quonset hut, 1949. As **SUZANNE** *watches* **HAMPSHIRE** *lecture she becomes excited, leaning forward listening to him more intently than ever.)*

HAMPSHIRE. The idea of Chance only reminds the reader of the sphere of ideal possibilities of what ought to be happening but is not. The illusion of freedom diminishes in the course of Hardy's novels. The net narrows and finally closes.

Inherent in almost all Hardy's characters are those natural instincts which become destructive because social convention suppresses them, attempting to make the human spirit conform to the "letter." Hardy absorbs Tess's personal situation into a vast system of causation.

(SCENE ENDS.)

SUZANNE. *(Present)* For a long time no one knew who the killer was. She was the one I had called Cathi. But that was later.
Before Christmas of my freshman quarter, Professor Hampshire wrote on my paper, "Make appointment to see me."

(SCENE: English office. SUZANNE and HAMPSHIRE, 1949.)

SUZANNE. His office in the English Department was along a path beyond the Oval. I seldom walked there and once I left the Oval I got lost on the streets on that side of the campus and was almost late for my four o'clock appointment. It was dark. He was sitting in a greyish office with several empty desks.

(SCENE: English office. SUZANNE enters in saddle oxfords, skin, matching sweater, cloth woolen coat. Again she wears powder blue, a popular color in 1949.)

SUZANNE. *(Present)* I was quite nervous. It was the first time a professor at Ohio State had asked to see me.

(In the office SUZANNE sits opposite HAMPSHIRE.)

SUZANNE. *(Present)* He was crouched over his desk writing and seemed smaller than in class, very pale, glasses, the same grayish woolen suit.

SUZANNE. *(In office.)* Professor Hampshire, you wrote on my paper you wanted to see me.

HAMPSHIRE. Oh yes, Suzanne, sit down, please. Did you bring your paper?

SUZANNE. Yes.

HAMPSHIRE. Let me see it.

SUZANNE. *(Present)* For a moment he seemed to forget me and read the brief paper in its entirety. For a moment watching him I realized he was a man of about thirty. I later was to discover he was a lecturer and this was his first year at Ohio State.

HAMPSHIRE. What is your major?

SUZANNE. I am undeclared. But if I do well this quarter I want to apply to take another English course in the spring, but I know I have to have special permission for further English courses.

SUZANNE. *(Present)* He didn't seem to hear me.

HAMPSHIRE. *(In his office.)* Did you write this paper yourself?

SUZANNE. Yes, Professor Hampshire.

HAMPSHIRE. What reference books did you use?

SUZANNE. I used no reference books. I wrote this paper late one night in the dorm, the night before it was due.

SUZANNE. *(Present)* He returned the paper to me, staring at the desk top. Suddenly he looked up.

HAMPSHIRE. Have you read Hardy before?

SUZANNE. *(Present)* He didn't seem to want to continue speaking. I tried to tell him that I wanted to study more English courses, how much I loved literature. But he stood up interrupting me. He didn't speak but gathered his books together. And stared at me, then nodded. I saw the conference was over.

(**SUZANNE** *stands in office, moves away staring back at* **HAMPSHIRE.**)

*(**OFFICE SCENE ENDS.**)*

*(**SCENE:** Stacks. From the window snow is falling.* **SUZANNE** *[Present] studies her paper.)*

(**SUZANNE** *[1949] walks across the Oval in darkness.*)

SUZANNE. *(Present)* I got lost again between two buildings behind University Hall.

Walking back in the darkness I remembered passages of my paper. And I remembered the comments Professor Hampshire had written on the margins.

SUZANNE. *(1949) (Stands on Oval.)*

"Paper conveys a profound feeling for the material."

"Paper has unusual empathy for Tess."

"The language of the paper seems an extension of Hardy's own language."

(She hears HAMPSHIRE *'s voice.)*

HAMPSHIRE. It's brilliant. It's brilliant.

(SCENE ENDS.)

(SCENE: Dorm. Lights on dark corridors and a dim small room lit by a single lamp.

IRIS ANN *is lying across the bed crying. Like* SUZANNE *she wears a pale skirt and sweater [possibly pink] and like Suzanne her hair is in a soft page boy.*

From the corridors we hear sounds of muffled laughing and talking.

SUZANNE *enters room.)*

SUZANNE. *(Present)* At the dorm my roommate, Iris Ann, was waiting for me to eat. Iris was lying on the bed crying. Her boyfriend had broken their engagement. We went down to the dining room and ate as usual at one of the tables where the Negro girls sat.

(SCENE IN DORM ENDS with SUZANNE *looking at* IRIS ANN.*)*

SUZANNE. *(Present)* After dinner we walked across the wet grass up to High Street. The path wound around a new structure half finished. We chattered. All except Iris Ann. After dinner it was not uncommon for us to go to Tomaine Tommy's and bring back cheeseburgers to be eaten later that night. On the way back to the dorm Iris started sobbing. It had begun to snow.

And often music came from the corridors. A song called "Don't Go Away Mad" was popular.

(Sound of music in the corridors.)

SUZANNE. *(Present)* In class the next week Professor Hampshire read again from Hardy.

(SCENE: Quonset hut. SUZANNE *stares up at* HAMPSHIRE.*)*

HAMPSHIRE. *(Reads.)* "... It was not until she was quite close that he could believe her to be Tess.

'I saw you – turn away from the station – just before I got there – and I have been following you all this way!'

She was so pale, so breathless, so quivering in every muscle, that he did not ask her a single question, but seizing her hand, and pulling it within his arm, he led her along. To avoid meeting any possible wayfarers he left the high road, and took a footpath under some firtrees. When they were deep among the moaning boughs he stopped and looked at her inquiringly.

'Angel,' she said, as if waiting for this, 'Do you know what I have been running after you for? To tell you that I have killed him!' A pitiful white smile lit her face as she spoke.

'What!' said he, thinking from the strangeness of her manner that she was in some delirium.

'I have done it – I don't know how,' she continued. 'Still, I owed it to you, and to myself Angel. I feared long ago, when I struck him on the mouth with my glove, that I might do it some day for the trap he set for me in my simple youth, and his wrong to you through me. He has come between us and ruined us, and now he can never do it any more. I never loved him at all, Angel, as I loved you. You know it, don't you? You believe it? You didn't come back to me, and I was obliged to go back to him. Why did you go away – why did you – when I loved you so? I can't think why you did it. But I don't blame you; only, Angel, will you forgive me my sin against you, now I have killed him? I thought as I ran along that you would be sure to forgive me now I have done that. It came to me as a shining light that I should get you back that way. I could not bear the loss of you any longer – you don't know how entirely I was unable to bear your not loving me! Say you do now, dear, dear husband; say you do, now I have killed him!'

'I do love you, Tess – O, I do – it is all come back!' he said, tightening his arms round her with fervid pressure. 'But how do you mean – you have killed him?'

'I mean that I have,' she murmured in a reverie.

'What, bodily? Is he dead?'

'Yes. He heard me crying about you, and he bitterly taunted me; and called you by a foul name; and then I did it. My heart could not bear it.'"

(SUZANNE cries.

HAMPSHIRE *glances at her. He leaves quonset hut. She remains in her seat.)*

*(**SCENE ENDS.**)*

(Dorm music.)

SUZANNE. *(Present)* One by one the white girls went to live on The Row. Their pattern was to live in the dorm their freshman year and then go live in The House. Although we had sororities, Alpha Kappa Alpha and Delta Sigma Theta, we did not have "houses." We met in rooms on campus or in private homes. So we remained in the dorm.

*(Dorm music. **SUZANNE** [1950] sitting in dorm room.)*

SUZANNE. Sorority Row right off High Street seemed a city in itself: the cluster of streets with the columned mansions sitting on top of the lawn appeared like a citadel.

SUZANNE. *(Reads her book of symbols.)* "A city should have a sacred geography never arbitrary but planned in strict accord with the dictates of a doctrine that the society upholds."

(SCENE ENDS.)

SUZANNE. *(Present)* I never walked on those blocks and saw them only from Mrs. Tyler's coupe. There was no reason for Negroes to walk in those blocks.

(SCENE: University Hall, 1950. **IRIS ANN** *and* **SUZANNE** *watch vivid footage of film* Potemkin.*)*

SUZANNE. *(Present)* Before she dropped out of Ohio State, Iris Ann wanted to be a music major. She had been first violinist in her high school orchestra. She told me some of the music students went to University Hall to a film society. We went a few times, walking across the Oval in the rain and saw a movie called *The Battleship Potemkin.* The movie was shown on the ground level of the hall. Down the massive stairwells with iron flowered balustrades we walked to a small auditorium.

I had never seen a movie as old as that. There were two showings. We went back to see the other half.

SUZANNE. *(At Potemkin.)* Who is Eisenstein?

SUZANNE. *(Present)* Iris Ann said she would ask one of the music students, Sonia. Sonia gave Iris Ann a typed paragraph on a small piece of paper describing the movie.

(SUZANNE [1950] and **IRIS ANN** *continue watching Potemkin.)*

SUZANNE. *(Present) (Reads paper.)* "Battleship Potemkin concentrates on the mutiny on a battleship of the Black Sea Fleet during the 1905 Revolution with the massacre on the Odessa steps. Down a seemingly endless flight of steps march soldiers advancing on the fleeing citizens."

SUZANNE. *(Present)* There was more on the scenes I had been drawn to.

(**SUZANNE** *and* **IRIS ANN** *continue watching film.*)

SUZANNE. *(Present) (Reads paper.)* "The storming of the Winter Palace, the dismemberment of the Tsar's Statue and a dead horse caught at the top of an opening drawbridge."

When we went back to see the second half I tried to remember what I had read. I asked Iris Ann were any of her music students there. She said she had seen one down front of the auditorium. I went to the library and tried to find out more about "this Eisenstein."

For some reason the crumpled bit of paper Sonia had given Iris Ann about *Potemkin* became important to me. I kept it in the top desk drawer in my room and would unfold it and read it over.

SUZANNE. *(At* Potemkin, **SUZANNE** *studies film.) Battleship Potemkin* concentrates on the mutiny on a battleship of the Black Sea Fleet during the 1905 Revolution with the massacre on the Odessa Steps... the storming of the Winter Palace... the dismemberment of the Tsar's statue...

(SCENE ENDS.)

SUZANNE. *(Present)* Iris Ann could play the violin beautifully. And sometimes she'd go into the study room at the end of the corridor and practice. I asked her about the courses she was taking. They're all theory, she said. Sue, I just like to play. I've studied since I was eight at the Institute. But here courses are all theory. She studied the theory books often on Saturday and Sunday.

Her uncle, a well-known doctor from Akron, came to visit us one Sunday. He made Iris Ann come out of the study room. That department is putting you under too much pressure, he said. I don't think they want you.

I became pregnant the following Christmas, 1950. My parents thought I spent the last day of my break with Iris in Akron but I had come back to Columbus and spent two days with Bobby above the ravine.

(SCENE: Path near quonset hut, 1950s.)

SUZANNE. *(Present)* I had not seen him after the spring quarter ended. In fact, I did not see him until the next fall in 1950. I had applied to be an English major but had been denied. They let me take a trial course on Shaw, Wilde, Moliere. I had seen Professor Hampshire on his way to the quonset hut.

SUZANNE: I am taking a trial course.

HAMPSHIRE. It's a shame.

SUZANNE. *(Present)* The previous quarter I had taken his course on Beowulf Again he had liked my papers.

HAMPSHIRE. *(On path.)* It's not necessary for you to take a trial course. It's a shame.

(SCENE ENDS.)

SUZANNE. *(Present)* He hurried on.

On that same path in one year we would meet.

It was February 1951 when I told him I was pregnant. He was on the same walkway that led to the hut. Within the quonset I could see students gathering. I had not seen him since December, when I had gone to his house above the ravine.

On that cold morning I stopped him as he came toward me. I had been waiting for him as he came up the steps of University Hall and onto the Oval. The immense circle of buildings was majestic amid dark trees and snow.

I told him I was pregnant.

(SCENE: Path near quonset hut.)

SUZANNE: *(Hardly audible.)* I am pregnant.

SUZANNE. *(Present)* He stopped an instant.

HAMPSHIRE. *(On path.)* That's not possible. We were only together twice. You surely must have other relationships. It's not possible.

SUZANNE. *(Present)* He walked past me.

HAMPSHIRE. I don't have time to talk to you, Sue. I'm giving a talk in University Hall Thursday at eight o'clock. Wait for me afterward, perhaps we can talk.

SUZANNE. *(Present)* He left me standing at the edge of the Oval.

(SCENE ENDS.)

SUZANNE. *(Present)* I remained in the dorm until March when I was expelled. The head of the dorm, Miss Dawson, read my diaries to the dormitory committee and decided I was unsuitable. I did not fit into campus life. And after the baby was born I would not be allowed to return to the campus.

Miss D. had gone into my room and found my poems, my Judy Garland records, my essay on loneliness and race at Ohio State and the maps I had made likening my stay here to that of Tess's life at the Vale of Blackmoor.

She called me to her office at the top of the stairs. She was a spinster and walked with a cane.

(SCENE: SUZANNE talking to MISS DAWSON in her office.)

(MISS DAWSON is a thin, white-haired woman wearing a dark coat sweater. She carries a cane.)

MISS DAWSON. I have observed you sitting alone behind the dorm. The committee read your notes on T. S. Eliot and Richard Wright. You will not be allowed to re-enter.

(SCENE ENDS.)

SUZANNE. *(Present)* March 17, 1951, was my last day in the dorm. I was three months pregnant.

My parents were humiliated. My father was a well-known Cleveland minister. They sent me to New York. I stayed with my aunt, my father's sister. She was a music teacher who had never married. She lived in Harlem. Those were the saddest months of my life.

My babies were born the beginning of September in Harlem Hospital, September 2, 1951.

My aunt begged me to stay in New York. I didn't know why but I wanted to return to Columbus. Finally Aunt Louise remembered a friend she had known when she went to Spelman who lived in Columbus. Her friend was Mrs. Tyler, a widow who boarded students in her large house near Long Street.

I took my baby daughters and boarded the train. Aunt Louise came to Grand Central. She cried.

AUNT LOU'S VOICE. Sue, please stay here.

SUZANNE. *(Present)* But I wanted to return. My parents hadn't spoken to me. But they gave me money. I settled in with Mrs. Tyler. It was agreed I would care for my daughters in the daytime and in the afternoon from four o'clock to nine o'clock I got a job as a department store stock girl. Mrs. Tyler asked me no questions. She knew

Louise Carter was my aunt. Before my aunt became a music teacher she had had a short career as a singer. She sang in local churches as well as at concerts of Negro groups.

(SCENE: SUZANNE *sitting in dimly lit sewing room, holding twins.)*

SUZANNE. *(Present)* My twins were three months old when I returned to Columbus.

It had been a year since I had gone to Bobby's home. I remembered his wall of recordings. He talked about Mozart, one of his favorite books was *Elizabethan World Picture.* He had given me a copy. Often I would meditate on repetitive phrases:

SUZANNE: *(In sewing room.)* Chain of being

Sin

the Links in the Chain

the Cosmic Dance

SUZANNE. *(Present)* I had learned he was from New York. I had also learned he had gone to Fordham, and had been married briefly to an Indian woman. It was his first year at Ohio State when I entered his freshman class. He was twenty-nine.

The days were long caring for the babies. Sometimes Mrs. Tyler's neighbors shunned me.

(SEWING ROOM SCENE ENDS.)

SUZANNE. *(Present)* Iris Ann dropped out of school and went back to Akron. I remembered the early days of my pregnancy and how she had gone to the health center with me. The fall of my sophomore year my major became elementary education. After I received a "C" in the trial course on Wilde and Shaw I was told by the secretary in the English Department that I could take no further English courses. My professor had been a man called Hodgson, a tall man in his fifties. He was accompanied often by his assistant. He smiled a great deal but seldom talked to anyone. He gave me "C's" on every paper. When I told the secretary I'd like to talk to him, she said Professor Hodgson was not able to see any more students that quarter but I could make an appointment with his assistant.

So in the fall I declared elementary education and began taking courses on teaching children. How I missed the imagery, the marvel, the narratives, the language of the English courses.

The new courses made me depressed. I hated them.

I ran into Professor Hampshire at the bookstore on High Street. I told him how hard I had worked on my papers on Shaw. He suggested I leave one at his office. I went to his office twice before I went to his house after Christmas.

(SCENE: Dorm room

IRIS ANN *lying across bed.*

SUZANNE. *[1950] standing by doorway listening to music from corridor.)*

SUZANNE. *(Present)* Iris Ann had been the only person who knew I was pregnant. She was still sad over Artie and often we cried at night. The white girls gave parties in the dorm.

(Dorm music, OKLAHOMA.)

SUZANNE. *(Present)* But we were never invited. Often they played music from Broadway musicals, *Oklahoma, Carousel.* Iris Ann and I went to the movies.

(SCENE ENDS.)

SUZANNE. *(Present)* Easter was when I told my father that I had been dismissed from the dorm. He was sitting in the office at his church. Tears came into his eyes.

(SCENE: **SUZANNE** *in the coupe in the stadium holding the twins.)*

Now sometimes on Sunday when I thought the campus was empty, I'd put the twins in Mrs. Tyler's coupe and drive to the river or the stadium. Sometimes I'd sit in the stadium inside the car and try to figure out what I was going to do with my life. The twins were in blankets on the seat next to me. I'd hold their fingers and, exhausted, fall asleep.

(SCENE ENDS.)

SUZANNE. *(Present)* I continued my routine of working as a stock girl.

Finally one February evening I went to one of Bobby's lectures sitting far in the back of the auditorium. It was on King Arthur's death. Bobby read at length in the dimly lit auditorium.

(SCENE: Auditorium. SUZANNE watches HAMPSHIRE. Her appearance has changed. She is thinner and dressed in darker clothes.)

HAMPSHIRE. Arthur Vows Revenge

"Till the blood bespattered his stately beard.

As if he had been battering beasts to death.

Had not Sir Ewain and other great lords come up,

His brave heart would have burst then in bitter woe:

'Stop!' these stern men said, 'You are bloodying yourself!'

Your cause of grief is cureless and cannot be remedied.

You reap no respect when you wring your hands:

To weep like a woman is not judged wise.

Be manly in demeanor, as a monarch should,

and leave off your clamour, for love of Christ in Heaven!

'Because of blood,' said the bold King, 'abate my grief

Before brain or breast burst, I never shall!

Sorrow so searing never sank to my heart;

It is close kin to me, which increases my grief.

So sorrowful a sight my eyes never saw.

Spotless, he is destroyed by sins of my doing!'

Down knelt the King, great care at his heart,

Caught up the blood carefully with his clean hands,

Cast it into a kettle-hat and covered it neatly,

Then brought the body to the birthplace of Gawain.

'I pledge my promise,' then prayed the King,

'To the Messiah and to Mary, merciful Queen of Heaven,

I shall never hunt again or unleash hounds

At roe or reindeer ranging on earth,

Never let greyhound glid or goshawk fly.'"

Arthur's only expression of sin in the poem is touched off by his grief over Gawain. But perhaps it was a battle-sin of caution, in that but for being "loth to make land across the low water" Arthur would have been at Gawain's side in the battle.

SUZANNE. *(Present)* I didn't know whether Bobby knew anything of what had happened to me. And I had no way of knowing that he was often following me.

(AUDITORIUM SCENE ENDS.)

AUNT LOU'S VOICE. Forget about that white man.

SUZANNE. *(Present)* Aunt Lou always said:

AUNT LOU'S VOICE. And forget about your parents. I don't know how my brother can ignore his own daughter. But, Sue, I have a little money saved. I'm going to help you go back to school.

SUZANNE: *(Present)* Seeing Bobby read made me brood over how he had dismissed me. Why?

I often thought of the second course I took with him the winter quarter of my freshman year.

We read *Beowulf.*

He spoke so eloquently of *Beowulf,* then read from it in old English.

Then it happened. Near the beginning of March, Robert Hampshire kidnapped and murdered our daughter. She was the one called Cathi. He drowned her in the ravine.

For a year detectives questioned me. Did I have enemies? Had I ever observed anyone following me?

At that time they didn't ask me about Cathi's father. Aunt Lou said if they ever did she had a former student who lived in Mt. Vernon, New York, and she had already discussed it with him. He would be glad to say he was the twins' father.

He was a young man Aunt Lou had helped a great deal and had even loaned him money to start his own cleaners. He was devoted to her.

For a while they seemed to think I knew who the murderer was.

I told him the only odd thing I remembered. Once I had been sitting in the car with my daughters by the river, had for a moment closed my eyes and fallen asleep, and awoke to the sound of someone running away from the car, someone who may have been looking in the window. And I did not drive to the river again. Then:

(*SCENE: Outside the doctor's office. Snow.* **SUZANNE** *is dressed in a dark coat. The babies lie in white bassinets. She takes the baby through a doorway. The baby coughs violently. She reappears in the falling snow and reaches into the car for the other twin.*

The twin is gone.)

SUZANNE. *(Present)* Then there had been a snowstorm. I was worried because Carol had a bad cough and I drove the babies to the doctor's office on Long Street. I pulled the coupe up into a side entrance. The offices were in a large, old-fashioned house. In the heavy snow I pulled the car as close to the door as possible. The babies were in white bassinets. Mrs. Tyler had offered to go with me. But she wasn't feeling well herself. It was snowing hard.

I took Carol into the lobby first and just as I laid her down on the chair she started to cough violently. I held her close. And then laid her back into the bassinet. I told the receptionist I had to get Cathi. I left both the lobby door and the car door open for those seconds. I turned and stepped outside into the falling snow and the few feet to the car. The car door was open, the white bassinet lay on the seat. But Cathi was gone.

(*SCENE ENDS.*)

SUZANNE. *(Present)* The detectives felt positive they knew who the murderer was.

Aunt Lou came to Columbus to be with us. I asked her did she think I should get Professor Hampshire to help.

"No," she said, "that would serve no purpose." She was the only person who knew Bobby was the father of my girls.

And as far as I know she never told anyone, not even my parents.

For weeks Aunt Lou sat with me in the cold house.

The police would say little but my aunt finally was able to find out that a man called Thurman, who had been in the penitentiary and often walked on campus posing as a student, was suspected. The police told my aunt they felt I knew more than I said and what did she really know about the life I led.

AUNT LOU'S VOICE. *(1951)* You don't understand. My niece is a sweet girl. A very sweet girl. All you white people are alike. You think because we're Negroes that my niece is mixed up in something shady. My niece knows no Thurman.

SUZANNE. *(Present)* She later told me she'd discovered this Thurman had been involved in several petty crimes on campus and in the campus area but also appeared to know many students and told the police he had seen me.

My aunt would not leave me, so in the summer we went back to New York. In the fall I returned to Columbus. I felt my baby's murderer was someone I knew.

(Brief past image of BUNNY *and her friends coming along dark corridors giggling.)*

(SCENE: SUZANNE *alone in her dorm room reading Thomas Hardy. From time to time* BUNNY *and her friends are heard in the next room singing.)*

SUZANNE. *(Present)* Why I thought they were capable of murder I don't know but sometimes I suspected a group of girls who lived at the end of the corridor in the dorm. They had been headed by an overweight, dark-haired girl called Patricia "Bunny" Manley. She and her group refused to speak to Iris and me and accused us of stealing her watch from the women's lavatory. If they saw us coming down the corridor they would giggle and close their door. I hated them. Their way of laughing when they saw us coming into the lounge, then refusal to speak was a powerful language. It had devastated me. And then there had been the watch incident, an incident so disturbing, especially since I myself owned beautiful possessions and jewelry that my parents had given me on going away to school. Both my parents were college graduates (my father, Morehouse, my mother, Atlanta University). I hid in the room and read Thomas Hardy. I loved the language of the landscape.

SUZANNE: (*Still in dorm room.*) "Behind him the hills are open, the sun blazes down upon the fields so large as to give an unenclosed character to the landscape. The lanes are white, hedges low and plashed the atmosphere colorless. Here in the valley the world seems to be constructed upon a smaller, more delicate scale."

(SCENE ENDS.)

SUZANNE. *(Present)* I remember how I had grown to dread the blocks bound by the stadium, the High Street, the vast, modern, ugly buildings behind the Oval, the dark old Union that was abandoned by all except the Negro students. And too, we were spied upon by the headmistress. She made no secret of the fact that she examined our belongings. "That's our general practice," she said.

Bunny and her friends bragged often to the maids that Iris and I had nothing in common with them, that there was nothing to talk about with us. I felt such danger from them. Had they somehow sought out me and my babies? Of course I told no one this. But I knew whites had killed Negroes, although I had not witnessed it. Thoughts of secret white groups murdering singed the edge of the mind.

I was often so tense that I wound the plastic pink

curlers in my hair so tightly that my head bled. When I went to the university health center the white intern tried to examine my head and at the same time not touch my scalp or hair.

"You're probably putting curlers in your hair too tightly," he said, looking away.

Now I remembered my father's sermons on lynching and the photographic exhibits we often had in our church of Negroes hanging from trees.

Then I met David. He would come by and say hello to Mrs. Tyler. When he discovered Carol was my child he made every effort to talk to me. He sensed my sorrow. When he found out that Cathi had been tragically killed he started to come by every evening after he left the law library. He asked no questions but only treated me with such great tenderness.

Finally I told him of everything. My pregnancy, my expulsion, the murder, and how I had returned to Columbus to see if I could find the murderer of my daughter.

I did not tell him yet of Bobby.

In the next months David and I spent many happy hours talking.

The police now referred to Cathi's drowning as the Ravine Murder.

Aunt Lou wrote and still encouraged me to leave Columbus. By this time David had proposed to me. He was from Washington.

(SCENE: **DAVID** *and* **SUZANNE** *sitting in* **MRS. TYLER'***s parlor.)*

SUZANNE. *(Present)* He told me how much I would love his family, particularly his younger sister, Alice, who he said was so much like me. She was studying literature at Howard (read several books at a time) and was also absolutely in love with the movies. He laughingly told me how she wrote brief plays as a hobby and how she'd come home from a movie and get members of her family to act out scenes from them.

He said her favorite movie star was Bette Davis, who she could not only imitate but also had made herself copies of Davis's dresses from Dark Victory, Now Voyager, and The Letter.

He said she also knew a great deal of poetry and would recite Edgar Allan Poe, Shelley, and Langston Hughes.

He had told her about Carol. And she had already crocheted a white bib for her and was sending it along with butter cookies for us.

(PARLOR SCENE ENDS.)

SUZANNE. *(Present)* My aunt said I was very lucky. She encouraged me to look to the future now.

*(**SCENE:** Auditorium, past.)*

SUZANNE. *(Present)* I had seen Robert Hampshire. In the bookstore there was a notice that he was again reading from King Arthur. I went.

He seemed far paler and smaller than I remembered. He didn't seem like anyone I had known. He read as usual without looking up from the page. It was clear he felt disdain for the audience. And it was clear he was very agitated.

After he read he spoke of King Arthur and the abyss.

HAMPSHIRE. The abyss in any form has a fascinating dual significance. On one hand it is a symbol of depth in general; on the other a symbol of inferiority. The attraction of the abyss lies in the fact that these two aspects are inextricably linked together. Most ancient or primitive peoples have at one time or another identified certain breaks in the earth's surface or marine depth with the abyss. The abyss is usually identified with the land of the dead, the underworld, and is hence though not always associated with the Great Mother and earth god cults. The association between the netherworld and the bottom of seas or lakes explains many aspects of legends in which palaces or beings emerge from an abyss of water. After King Arthur's death his sword thrown into the lake by his command is caught as it falls and before being drawn to the bottom flourished by a hand which emerges from the waters.

(SCENE ENDS.)

SUZANNE. *(Present)* David and I had begun plans to marry. He bought me a ring at Hoensteins.

Many people at Ohio State assumed that Val was the father of my twins. But Val and I never had an intimate relationship. When he discovered I was pregnant he just stopped calling. "I'm surprised," he told Iris Ann. "I really am surprised."

Like my parents he just could not believe this had happened to me. He didn't, like them, really want to know anything further. With my preference for Peter Pan blouses and precise straightened curls I had been almost a cliche of the ultimate virgin. I had totally believed sex was a sin before marriage.

(SCENE: **MRS. TYLER**'s *parlor.* **SUZANNE** *and* **VAL.** **SUZANNE** *holds* **CAROL** *in her arms.)*

SUZANNE. *(Present)* When Cathi was murdered he came to Mrs. Tyler's.

VAL. *(In* **MRS. TYLER**'s *parlor.)* Is it true it was your child that was murdered?

SUZANNE: Yes.

VAL. It's all so difficult to believe.

SUZANNE. *(Present)* He had brought me a box of chocolates. For when we had gone out to the freshman parties he often gave me a box of Whitman or Fanny Farmer chocolates.

VAL. Why don't you leave Columbus, Sue?

SUZANNE: I think I can eventually find out who killed my baby if I stay.

VAL. If I were you I'd leave. Most people at State think you left after you got pregnant, they think you went to New York.

SUZANNE. *(Present)* I saw how uncomfortable he was sitting on Mrs. Tyler's stiff couch. I held Carol in my arms. He seemed afraid to look at her.

SUZANNE. *(1951)* *(In* MRS. TYLER*'s parlor.)* Thank you, Val, for coming by.

SUZANNE. *(Present)* He stood and went to the door. Finally he glanced at Carol, frowned, and left.

VAL. (In the parlor.) Good bye, Sue.

(SCENE ENDS.)

SUZANNE. *(Present)* I often remembered Bunny and her friends had given the illusion of withholding secrets.
I had found a book about symbols on the bottom shelf of the bookstore on High Street. Often on a bottom shelf near the door there were assorted books and portfolios for sale. It was there I discovered several out-of-print soft-cover books on the French Impressionists. I bought one on Cézanne. And hung a print in my room. It was of the port of Marseilles. I studied the blues, reds, and yellows. It was the brightest color in the dorm with its dark furniture.

(SCENE: SUZANNE, *past, in dorm room reading book of symbols.)*

SUZANNE. *(Present)* Bunny and her friends in the closed room next door had become something I thought of a great deal. Their refusal to talk to me made me feel that they knew something about me that was not apparent to myself.

SUZANNE: *(Still in dorm room.)* "Secrets," my book on symbols said, "symbolize the power of the supernatural and this explains their disquieting effect upon most human beings."

SUZANNE. *(Present)* My little book of symbols that I had

bought on sale became precious to me.

I remembered again that during the quarter that I had taken the trial course I became very quiet.

(SCENE ENDS.)

SUZANNE. *(Present)* The police also suspected a neighbor of Mrs. Tyler's, but David, Aunt Louise, and Mrs. Tyler all said it had to be a stranger.

Alice, his sister, David said, was crocheting another bib; this one was pale yellow.

It was spring. Two years had passed since I lived in the dorm.

David and Mrs. Tyler told me every day that all this would be resolved and that one day the police would discover who had followed me in the snow.

Right after Easter Mrs. Tyler told me a grad student from Ohio State was coming that evening. He was doing a study of Negroes in the Columbus area and had heard from campus housing that she kept students and was also a native of Columbus and knew a great deal about the depression years there and the development of the neighborhoods.

When I left she was expecting him for an interview and had made cocoa.

David had gotten me a job in the law library in the stacks. The hours were 6:00 to 9:30. By 10:00 p.m. I was home. We saved money. David worked on two part-time jobs. Aunt Lou gave us something. That evening we pulled the car out of the drive at 5:20 to go to the law library. When we returned at 10:05 the Ohio State murders had occurred.

Robert Hampshire (posing as a researcher) had killed Carol, our twin, and himself. It seems that once inside Mrs. Tyler's living room he told her he was the father of the twins, that he had never been able to forget their existence. They ruined his life. He said he knew that one day I would reveal this, that he would be investigated, there would be tests and his whole career would fail.

He admitted he had waited for me outside the doctor's office and had taken Cathi. He told her he tried to follow the advice of his father who lived near London who had told him to just ignore me but he had been unable to do that. He was quite mad, she said, and had pushed her into the hallway and down the cellar stairs. When her son returned at 8:55 he found her crying and injured on the dark stairwell. Upstairs in the small sewing room where Carol and I slept Robert had killed Carol and himself (with a knife he had taken from the kitchen sink).

(SCENE: Law library, past.)

SUZANNE. *(Present)* **DAVID** found me here in the stacks of the law library on level zero sorting definitions of words. He remembers...

SUZANNE: *(In the law library, past)* Abyss, bespattered, cureless, misfortune, enemy, alien host, battle groups fated to fall on the field today.

(SCENE ENDS.)

SUZANNE. *(Present)* For many months I made drawings of the corridors in the dorm with the doors of each room outlined in red ink and muttered definitions of rooms, stains, color, skin.

I wrote long passages about my scalp and how it had bled and how I had examined my pores in a magnifying glass. And how the spots on the pillow cases had frightened me so that I had hidden my pillow cases even from Iris Ann.

But it seems the maid in the dorm corridor had told Miss D. that my pillow cases were stained. And they had examined the cloth together.

I thought I would die. David told me years later that he believed I was unable to go on. His parents and sister prepared a room for me in their house in Washington on 16th Street. It overlooked a part of Rock Creek Park. It was Alice's room. She gave it to me. It was a large, pale, cream-colored room with an arch and lovely windows. I didn't leave that room for months.

David and I were married the following year. I remained in Washington living with his family in the big old house on 16th Street. His father was a lawyer with the NAACP. In a year David finished law school at Ohio State.

The university protected Robert Hampshire for a long time. Nothing of the story came out in the papers. There were stories that a white professor had wandered into the Negro section of Columbus and was killed.

But years later I heard Robert Hampshire's father had come from London at the time. My father, who knew the state politicians, had also put pressure on the papers to bury the tragedy. He convinced them it was best for me.

Mrs. Tyler and her son stuck to the story that a researcher had come to the house, had gone into a fit of insanity, and that was all they knew. Within days the stories were confused.

David, Aunt Lou, and David's family told me nothing. Not even that my mother had been hospitalized.

Before today I've never been able to speak publicly of my dead daughters.

Good-bye, Carol and Cathi.

Good-bye...

(Pause.)

And that is the main source of the violent imagery in my work. Thank you.

(Lights bright on hundreds of books in stacks and on the window, falling snow.)

PROPS

FURNITURE
Library Table
Armless Chair
2 Seater Sofa/Bench
Upholstered Bench/Day Bed
Table Lectern

HAND PROPS
Presentation Notes
Picture of David Running
Lecture Notes I
Tess of the D 'Urbervilles Book
Indications of Place Names from *Tess.*
Lecture Notes II
Paper or Notepads on Table
Suzanne's Term Paper on *Tess.*
Book of Symbols
Notes on *Battleship Potemkin*
Cane
Briefcase
Notes on *King Arthur*
Thomas Hardy Book
Lecture Notes III on *King Arthur*
Box of Candy
Pencil for Young Suzanne
Composition Book for Young Suzanne
Pen for Hampshire.
School book bag for Young Suzanne

COSTUMES

The costumes are strictly early 1950's with the exception of Suzanne (Present).

SUZANNE ALEXANDER (Present) – Pale soft blouse, a skirt (also soft fabric and dark), and flat shoes.

SUZANNE ALEXANDER (1949-1952)/ **IRIS ANN** – wear saddle oxfords, flared skirts, sweater sets (powder blue, pink or yellow), fake strands of pearls, and pale flared winter coats. Hair in page boy cuts.

ROBERT HAMPSHIRE – Grey suit with vest, white shirt and tie.

DAVID ALEXANDER – Navy overcoat, navy suit, tie with a darker shirt.

VAL – Dark overcoat.

MISS DAWSON – Large grey sweater and a grey skirt.

www.ingramcontent.com/pod-product-compliance
Lightning Source LLC
Jackson TN
JSHW081419040825
88762JS00020B/191